I0538325

Opening Day

Daniel Arthur Smith

Opening Day

ISBN: 0988649322
ISBN-13: 978-0-9886493-2-3

Second Edition

Edited By
Crystal Watanabe

Also Written by Daniel Arthur Smith

The Cameron Kincaid Adventures
The Cathari Treasure
The Somali Deception

The Literary Fiction Series
The Potter's Daughter
Opening Day: A Short Story

The Horror Series
Agroland

* * * * *

For my Grandfather
&
To all of the other
Grandfathers, Fathers, & Grandsons, that have hunted
here and abroad.
&
For Susan, Tristan, & Oliver, as all things are.

* * * * *

.

OPENING DAY

To rouse the Boy, his Grandfather said one word, "Son."

The Boy flashed his heavy lids open to the hazy silhouette stepping away from his door. He rose from his bed knowing his Grandfather would not darken the doorframe with a second invitation.

Dawn was hours away. A nauseating miasma of coffee, corned beef hash, and cooking grease saturated the house.

The night before, layers of cedar-scented attire, retrieved from the recesses of the hall closet, had been folded by his bedside. The Boy dressed as rehearsed. The long john thermal underwear he slept in was now a second skin that made the denim jeans, which usually fit perfectly, uncomfortably snug. The soft red and black wool flannel hugged his shoulders too tightly. The Boy slipped thick grey woolen socks over his feet. The socks were new for his trip into the woods. These socks had been chosen off the Kmart rack for the broad red bands around the ankles. Unlike the thin yellow stripes on his white gym socks, he thought the red bands were appropriate for the occasion, almost formal. The socks not only felt good on his feet, they also made him feel warm inside. They were hunter's socks, socks for men.

After dressing, the Boy sat with his hands pressed flat beside him on the bed. He had rushed up and now a wave of grogginess disoriented him. The warm spot where he had been sleeping moments before beckoned him back. Afraid that sleep would grab him once his head hit the soft pillow, the Boy resisted. Spreading his fingers outward, he stretched his arms high above his head. A yawn began to overtake him. To combat the drowsiness, he forced the yawn to a sigh; the result was a heavy shudder. He shook his head loosely and rapidly shuttered his eyelids a few times to be certain he had chased away the temptation of sleep.

From the nightstand, the Boy took the suede leather case Mother had made for him and removed the folded buck knife. Thumb pressed on the locking mechanism, he unfolded and then inspected the blade for possibly the hundredth time since Grandfather had given him the knife the day before. Last night, the Boy had sharpened the blade three different times against the small companion bench stone, each time testing the fine metal edge on strips of newspaper. The final time he attempted to split a strand of his hair, though there had not been enough light to prove or disprove success. Now satisfied that the knife was ready, he carefully returned the blade to the folded position. The buck knife locked with a click. The Boy tested the security of the lock with his fingertips, marveling at how tight the thin blade seated in the handle, then carefully slipped the soft case around his treasure and forced the small bundle into his tight front pocket.

The Boy joined the other hunters gathered in the living room. The stench of the coffee was not bothering him as much. New odors permeated this area of the house, gun oil, leather, and wafts of smoke from the crackling pine. The doors of the tall glass gun cabinet were unlocked. Splayed open gun cases, each displaying a polished rifle, surrounded the cabinet one in front of the other.

Grandfather and the great uncles said nothing to each other. They went about their actions routinely, knowing what preparations were needed from year after year of the early morning ritual. They wore variations of thick red wool pants with four finger wide suspenders strung over their long john thermals and, even though they were still indoors, heavy lined hunting caps. Stacked in sealed packs on the table were the blaze orange nylon vests the older men were to slip over their red wool coats. A new law required that the color saffron cover a percentage of the hunter's body during deer season for high visibility in the thicket. In a culture lacking robed monks, the color marketed as safety orange and blaze orange distinguished a hunter from all others. A man's uniform.

The Boy's new quilted hunting suit and cap were blaze orange. The puffy pants and jacket were sized for a small man and pulled loosely over his jeans, an outer shell to the already too hot suffocating layers below.

Grandfather pulled long laces over the hooks of thigh high leather boots.

Grandfather's dog Doby, a Greyhound and Doberman mix, sniffed and licked at Grandfather's fingers while he laced. Grandfather most always had one of his three dogs near him. He preferred the company of dogs to that of his own species. Grandfather's bedroom was shelved with little canine statuettes given to him by family and friends over the years and on one wall hung a large green tapestry of Dogs Playing Poker. His dogs slept with him, ate with him at the table, and rode in his heavy trucks when he travelled to worksites across the county. The Boy's grandmother did not share her husband's sentiment toward canines, particularly when the dogs ate at the table, and of all the animals, she despised Doby the most.

Uncle Royce, Grandfather's brother, came in from the kitchen with two small plates. He held one out for the Boy. Breakfast was a pile of corned beef hash under a runny egg and a chunk of hard crust bread. The Boy accepted the plate without a word. The hash was gamy and loose from the egg. Each bite stayed in his mouth too long and made him think of snot. He forced himself to swallow. It was too early in the morning for his stomach to take in food, but the Boy ate as heartily as he could. Having only ever eaten corned beef hash with Grandfather gave the diced meat the distinction of being men's food. This was a hunter's breakfast and as disgusted as the Boy was, he relished sharing morning meal with the older men.

Grandfather and the Boy's great uncles were veterans of the wars against the Nazis and the Japanese. He imagined them in a black and white history culminated from Sunday afternoon movies and the nostalgic stories they had told him about themselves, each other, and men they referred to that he had never met, yet felt he should have. Uncle Royce had lost a thumb island hopping in the Pacific and Grandmother's brothers, Uncle Dick and Uncle Bob, had lost a finger and a thumb respectively, overseas in Europe somewhere. The Boy did not know exactly how all of these digits had been lost. He had been told they were shot off. Uncle Royce and Uncle Bob had other wounds as well, including a groin shot. The Boy never asked about the wounds, yet when he played with the other boys at school, throwing milkweed pod grenades and jerking sticks back and forth while making what they thought were machine gun sounds, he imagined fighting alongside Grandfather and his uncles as they must have been in their youth. In his mind, they were noble and all-knowing heroes. The Boy suspected their career as soldiers gave them some military insight into the morning preparation as he watched them ready themselves and their gear.

Uncle Bob filled a large metal hand warmer with lighter fluid and next to him on the sofa sat Uncle Dick, stroking the barrel of a 30-06 with an oiled cloth. After lacing his boots, Grandfather had also taken a rifle from a leather case and was polishing the lens of the scope.

Grandfather has many rifles. Today he's hunting with the 300 Savage. Grandfather had told the Boy that the crosshairs only needed to line up with the ear of a buck and the 300 would take most of the head clean off without wasting any meat. The thought alarmed the Boy. Targeting the heart was for trophy hunters, Grandfather had explained, and would damage the shoulders and ribs. Each member of the family made the effort to instill in the Boy that there was nothing noble in trophy hunting or stuffed heads on the wall. You could not eat a trophy. With loathing in their voices, they spoke of the hunters who came up from the flatland to drink away the week in their hunting camps. Hunting camp was a euphemism for playing cards, alcohol consumption, and reckless behavior. To see carcasses strapped to the hood of a car or hung on a pole downtown to show off the size of the buck while the meat slowly rotted disgusted them, as did hunters that ignored the code of conservation by making no distinction between a doe and a buck in the hunt. Grandfather shot at least one large buck every year and what he took from the field was immediately butchered and put into the freezer, never on display.

The Boy's family had hunted on the same property for over a hundred years for the sole purpose of obtaining food, plain and simple.

"Get your boots on," the Boy's grandfather told him. "Then get your gun ready."

The Boy was quick to act, pulling his large rubber snow boots from the side of the chair and pushing his feet eagerly into them. His gun had been cleaned the night before, yet Grandfather had taught him that the barrel was to be inspected before every use. The Boy went over to the gun case that had been assigned to him and slowly picked up the gun, careful not to let the barrel point away from the floor. He knew that his elders were monitoring every detail and action. The gun was heavy and massive to him. This was on purpose. The Boy would not be going out into the woods with a rifle like the men. He would take the old twelve-gauge shotgun just as, for generations, every member of his family had on their first hunt. The twelve-gauge was a beautiful weapon with a hand carved stock and a large rubber pad on the butt. He racked the pump action on the shotgun twice to be sure nothing was in the chamber and then checked the barrel slowly and methodically, just as Grandfather had shown him. When the Boy finished, everyone else was zipping up their gun cases, so he did the same.

Uncle Dick tilted his mug bottom high to finish his coffee and then was the first to put on his heavy jacket. In moments, they were lined up at the door with their gun cases under their arms, thermoses and mugs in hand.

"Here, put these in your pockets," said Grandfather. He gave the Boy a wadded up handful of empty plastic bread bags.

"What are these for?" asked the Boy.

"You'll need them to put the heart and liver in when you get your deer," said Uncle Royce.

"Oh," said the Boy. He stuffed the bags into the pockets of his jacket.

Grandfather opened the door and they filed out, Grandfather, Uncle Dick, Uncle Bob, and the Boy, followed by Uncle Royce, whose job was to push back the dogs crowding the door. The dogs would not be making this trip.

The dark sky showed no sign of morning. The brisk cold seized the Boy's face and hands. The cold air shot in through his nose and into the back of his throat. The iced layer on the snow crunched as the men marched across the porch and out to the driveway.

Of Grandfather's many vehicles, he had decided to take his white van. Uncle Dick and Uncle Bob would take Uncle Bob's car. Uncle Bob had started the car earlier so that the heater would have time to warm the interior. The engine of the car made a low rumble in the quiet morning and as the Boy walked close, he passed through the acrid vapor of exhaust that hung in the frigid air.

The van had not been started. The frost covering the windows reflected the light from the porch. Across the white paint on the side of the van, the Boy could see a crystalline film. Grandfather rolled open the side door and then slid his gun case behind the front seats. He took the Boy's case and told the Boy to climb in. The Boy's legs felt stiff in the thick layers of clothes and he fought against his own weight as he hoisted himself up into the van, plopping onto the makeshift bed in the back.

The interior of the van was an icebox. The Boy could see his breath forming in the cold air before him. With each breath, the cold reached further into his lungs.

Uncle Royce eased his gun case from under his arm, placed it on top of the others, and then opened up the passenger door. Leaning far in, he set a metal lunch bucket and thermos in the gulf between the passenger and driver's seat and then grabbed the window scraper from the center console. Uncle Royce then shut all of the doors and began to scrape the windows. The scraping echoed in the van as the frost resisted the plastic edge. The frost loudly ripping from the window made the Boy feel uneasy and raised the hair on his neck in a cold chill. He reached into the back of his collar, pulled up his flannel, and then stretched his cap down around his ears.

The window beside him now clear, the Boy could see Grandfather standing outside the window of Uncle Bob's car. They were talking while Uncle Dick got into the passenger side. The Boy wanted Grandfather to hurry and for the first time this morning began to doubt if this was going to be as he imagined.

When Uncle Royce finished scraping, the Boy thought that would be a catalyst to getting Grandfather into the van, instead Uncle Royce walked over to the car. Uncle Royce raised his forearms in the air and began to motion them forward, as if guiding a plane into a landing. The men were now deciding where on the property they wanted to hunt and Uncle Royce was giving directions. The Boy had been with the men the afternoon before when they'd discussed sightings of particular bucks and now they were deciding where their best chances were at finding them this morning. The large property was over 600 acres, about a square mile, and there were many historically designated hunting areas that the Boy knew by name.

The Boy opened his mouth wide and huffed a cloud of steam. He chomped playfully at the mist in large bites. Though his hands were back in his pockets, they were still cold, so he dug out the balled up gloves.

Finally, Grandfather and Uncle turned toward the van. The Boy fixed his posture upright, not wanting to be seen as anything less than enthused. Grandfather and Uncle Royce got into the van and, after three attempts, started the engine. The heater fan sent a jet of cold air to the back of the van into the Boy's face, adding to the chill. The Boy scrunched up to take the cold and said nothing. Grandfather reached over to turn the fan down. A musty odor of mildew, suppressed by the cold before, now stirred in the air.

Uncle Bob's car pulled away in front of the van and did a k-turn in the wide driveway. As the Boy's uncles drove back and passed the van, Grandfather put the truck into gear, did a k turn as well, and then followed Uncle Bob's path out onto the road.

The property, which Grandfather referred to as the farm, was a few miles away from the Boy's grandparents' house on the river and took only a short time to reach. The farm had been the homestead of Grandfather's great-grandfather in the early 1800s. There were only remnants of what was once a farm on the property now. An ancient tractor was parked at the entranceway to the property, a rusted sentry guarding a two-track lane that ran back into the woods. Next to the two-track stood an old barn, greyed from years of weather, with the large doors unable to fully close. To the side of the barn was the elevated foundation of a large farmhouse that had burnt down when Grandfather was still a child.

Uncle Bob drove onto the two-track and Grandfather followed. The Boy watched the bright red taillights of

Uncle Bob's car bounce up and down as each vehicle drove slowly over the dirt trail's small hills and valleys, worn deep from the big trucks Grandfather usually drove to the back of the farm.

Just past the edge of the woods behind the barn, the car brake lights glared crimson. The Boy lurched forward when Grandfather abruptly stopped the van. Uncle Royce absently reached for the block of wood on the console, the dangling key silhouetted against the lights of the dash. The Boy watched Uncle Royce walk over to an I-beam at the edge of Uncle Bob's headlights. A steel cable that crossed the road began to move up and down and then fell to the ground.

Grandfather reached into his pocket and pulled out a handful of assorted hard candies in wax paper and plastic wrappers. In a mechanical loose toss, he spread the sweets onto the console and then in the same motion reached down for one.

"Here," said Grandfather. He handed a candy to the Boy.

The Boy took the candy. Useless in his clothed fingers, he removed his gloves to unwrap the wax paper. Grandfather shifted the van into gear and then rested his wrists on the steering wheel, unwrapping his own piece of candy while the van slowly pulled ahead of where the cable had fallen to the ground. The taillights of Uncle Bob's car continued bouncing up the trail ahead of them while Grandfather and the Boy waited for Uncle Royce to fasten the cable gate back to the steel girder. The Boy pressed the sweet against the roof of his mouth with his tongue. Immediately, the taste of butterscotch filled his mouth. His grandfather did not appear to the Boy to be a man that would enjoy sweets, yet he was already having another. When Uncle Royce got back into the van, they began to slowly go forward again.

The van not only bounced, the height and girth caused the truck to rock to the side as the wheels in turn sunk into the deep frozen wells. Ice crushed beneath the weight of the van as they rolled through. Sometimes the van would shift so radically that the Boy would lose balance and lean to the far right or left or the tires would fall so abruptly that his stomach would jar.

The van slowed to almost a stop and the Boy could see that they had caught up to his Uncle Bob. Ahead, there was a mixture of light and shadow of rushing water across the road.

"Beavers," said Grandfather.

The Boy knew that the stream would wash out the road from time to time because of the beavers. He had been with Grandfather when repairing the culvert that ran beneath the road and had been in the dump truck when they emptied fresh gravel out to replace what had been washed away. Uncle Royce had blown up the beaver dam with dynamite more than once. The thought of an explosion in the woods fed the Boy's imagination. Though he would have liked to, he had never seen the beaver dams, nor had he ever seen the dynamite. He imagined Uncle Royce, a large man, lighting a fuse and then running to duck for cover with his hands over his hat and ears. Since the Boy had never seen the giant of a man run, that part was always the hardest image to conjure.

Before the car in front of them had finished pushing through and out of the rushing water, Grandfather accelerated the van in anticipation. The axles of the van slamming against the dipping terrain caused the Boy to lift above the bed, the hard candy almost flying out of his mouth. Beyond the washout, the road ran up a steady incline with fewer potholes so the vehicles were able to maintain the momentum without the hazard of twisting a chassis.

When the Boy saw Uncle Bob's brake lights glare again, he knew they were close to the ridge.

The ridge was a vast clearing in the middle of the woods that ran almost a mile wide and a third of a mile across. The

Boy thought the ridge had originally been cropland for the farm. The clearing was now peppered with gravel pits for Grandfather's excavation business and Uncle Royce kept hives in the far corner.

The ridge was elevated high on the property. To the front was the low valley the van had driven through, mostly swamped by the beaver dams despite Grandfather and Uncle Royce's efforts. The back of the ridge was a mystery to the Boy where he had seen an old overgrown two-track that faded off into the woods, perhaps an old lumber trail, he thought, that once held as much purpose as the barn at the gate. During the summer, the Boy spent a lot of time on the ridge with Grandfather. While Grandfather worked the heavy equipment, the Boy would scour the property. He investigated frog ponds that filled some of the pits and the many old vehicles that had been towed there to rust. He imagined that the old overgrown faded two-track led to a ghost cabin, or a maybe a ghost town, or perhaps the path was an actual time machine that really would take someone to an earlier era.

At the mouth of the road where the clearing opened to the ridge, the car's headlights went dark and so did the lights of the van. The Boy did not know how Grandfather knew where to drive in the darkness beyond the windshield, but as they entered the ridge, he could see the outline of Uncle Bob's car against a faint indigo horizon of the open field. Uncle Bob turned to the right. The Boy supposed Uncle Bob was going to the edge of the ridge that overlooked the swamp. That is where Uncle Royce had last seen a large buck with a huge rack, at least eighteen points, he had said. The Boy had never seen a live buck with eighteen points. Grandfather drove forward and across the field to the back of the ridge. The Boy was finally going to see what was beyond the overgrown two-track that ghosted into the trees.

The lake of snow glowed outside the side windows of the van as the truck glided across the field up to the edge of the woods. The Boy's fingers were on the edge of the cushion. He wanted out of the van. Then with a turn of the key, the engine began to choke silent, not all at once, rather with a number of drawn out grunts from the exhaust punctuated by loud silence and stillness until nothing filled everything. The Boy pushed back with his palms and shifted his pupils side to side afraid to move his head, because from that moment every movement was to be stealth and measured.

Grandfather and Uncle Royce slowly opened their doors. The clicking of the door handles seemed amplified and each clink of metal upon metal was distinct and precise.

When the front doors opened, a rush of cool evergreen scent filled the van. The cedar trees on the back edge of the ridge were fast growing and to the left, manifested into a cedar swamp deep into the woods. The Boy could tell by the height of the young trees edging from the woods that the clearing was slowly being invaded, overtaken by the evergreens.

Uncle Royce opened the doors to the side of the van and the heat that had built up was replaced by bitter cold. The Boy realized how comfortable he had become during the short drive over. Standing slowly, he hunched forward and awkwardly made his way toward the door and out of the van, lowering himself onto the new fallen snow. During the short trip, he had also forgotten how cumbersome he had become in his new hunting suit. The Boy's stomach suddenly ached and he felt stiffer now than before, parts of his body seemed too hot, while his face and ungloved hands were cold and losing heat. As he started to slip his gloves back on, Grandfather tapped him on the shoulder and gestured him toward the back of the van. One of the van's back doors was already opened. Grandfather reached into the storage space below the bed and pulled out two handfuls of small apples. They were old and pungent, picked from the orchard trees across the ridge at least a month before. Grandfather stuffed some of apples into the Boy's pocket and then tossed one on the ground and crushed the fruit under his boot. He took the apple from the ground, rubbed the mealy pulp up and down on his jacket, and then rubbed the meat of the apple on the Boy. The musty odor was stronger now, sweet, yet off. After putting some apples into his own pocket, Grandfather filled a mildewed burlap potato sack with more of them, handed the sack to the Boy, and then pulled out a plastic bag of large carrots.

Grandfather eased the back door closed and then led the Boy back around to the side of the van. Uncle Royce already had his rifle out and was loading in a clip. Leaning into the van, Grandfather unzipped the remaining gun cases with two fast and faint buzzes as though he had caught a mad bee from each. He stood up from the van, holding a gun in each hand, the shotgun and the rifle both large compared to the 30-30 that Uncle Royce held. The Boy took the shotgun from Grandfather, his chest filling with pride as he felt the weight in his hand.

This was for real. The Boy was there with the men, each with a gun. The cold no longer bothered him.

Grandfather looked at the shotgun and then raised his brow at the Boy. The Boy lowered the barrel and, almost wobbling, kneeled toward the ground and set the sack of apples down. He checked the safety and stepped back from the van, letting his shoulders and chest fall with the weight of the shotgun tucked under his arm. When Grandfather was satisfied with the Boy's demeanor, he offered him a shotgun shell. The Boy had wanted a slug simply because the other boys in school had told stories about slugs. This shell held buckshot, and to the Boy, this was somehow lesser than the large hunk of metal that made up a slug. After taking the shell, he inserted the cartridge into the shotgun, then shifted his eyes back at Grandfather. Grandfather nodded, signaling permission to rack the shell into the chamber. The shotgun stayed pointed at the snow as he silently slid the pump toward him and then out again. The shotgun was loaded. He could feel himself breathing deeply. As he'd practiced again and again, the Boy checked once more to see that the metal safety button was in place, careful to keep the shotgun teetered on his forearm so that the barrel would pivot naturally and safely down toward the ground, keeping his finger judgment distance from the trigger.

Grandfather was putting a shell into the 300. Uncle Royce surely had a full clip. Grandfather and the Boy each had only one shell in their guns. Grandfather had told him that only one shot was needed to down a buck. "One shot, one kill. If you're unsure of the shot, afraid that you will miss, do not take the shot." The Boy wanted more than one shell, yet Grandfather had shot a buck every year that he could remember, so surely that would be all he should need.

As Uncle Royce and Grandfather finished doing what they needed at the van, the Boy focused on the trail. The dark shadows of the first rows of cedars were all he could make out against the glowing white snow.

Uncle Royce clipped a red plastic bean-filled heat seat from the van to his waist, and began to walk toward the cedars while Grandfather closed the side door. With the van closed up, there would be no turning back.

The Boy lowered his waist to pick up the apples, not wanting to bend over too far or wobble again. The risk of letting the barrel touch the ground was too great and would result in a scolding he did not want. He waited for his Grandfather to go forward a few steps before falling into rank.

The snow lightly covered the ground and the Boy's steps were awkward in the heavy rubber snow boots. A thick insulated liner fit into the rubber casing of the boots, and with his wool socks, the boots were foreign to his feet. Uncle Royce and Grandfather steadily moved forward and the Boy hurried to keep up. His gait was bowed and mechanistic, each thigh lifting the knee to suspend a boot in the air and propel his foot to the following step.

A light nausea filled the Boy's stomach and his head was hot. He wanted to adjust his cap, but to move his cap would mean the Boy would have to stop walking to keep his balance. Setting down the apples was too complicated of a maneuver, so he lifted his hand holding the bag and shoved the cap into another uncomfortable position. Uncle Royce and Grandfather were getting away from him, so he went forward another few steps before having to stop again, this time pushing the cap too close to his brow. Trying to correct the cap with the tip of his gloved fingers, he pushed the hat back too far, and he felt the elasticity slip up to the top of his head. The cap started to fall off, so he quickly pinned the hat between his hand and his head. Stuck with his hand in a salute, he pressed the cap against the side of his head, the apple sack resting on the side of his face. The mildewed burlap was cold and smelled terrible. If he dropped the cap on the ground he would have to bend over, and that would be no good. He knelt slowly down, his arm still to the side of his head, tilting gently back to keep the shotgun steady. Leaning his head to the side, he flopped the cap onto his glove and gently lowered the sack down to the ground. He attempted to keep the top of the sack from collapsing inward so he would not have to reach farther down to retrieve the bag. The Boy gripped and then placed the cap on the center top of his head and gently pulled at the edges to a secure position. After successfully fitting the cap, he reached down again for the sack of apples, feeling for the burlap with his fingertips.

Grandfather looked back in his direction and then stopped.

Grandfather peered at the Boy crouched in the snow with his head tilted to the side. In the dim light, the Boy could make out what he thought was a scowl on Grandfather's face. The Boy slowly raised his body and Grandfather waived his hand for the Boy to come forward. When the Boy was close, Grandfather and Uncle Royce turned and continued into the woods.

The Boy kept up with the older men with some effort. A short way up the trail, Grandfather and Uncle Royce both froze. The Boy's eyes went wide. He still had a knee raised so he decided to let his boot continue forward to rest in the snow. Grandfather raised a flat hand to his side, signaling the Boy not to move. Standing on one foot, a burlap sack of apples in one hand, and a twelve-gauge shotgun in the other, the Boy strained to peer through the darkness in front of them, seeing nothing except faint illusory apparitions. The only sound he could hear was his own breathing, so he held his breath as not to be scolded by either of the men. The three stood motionless long enough for the Boy to become physically uncomfortable. He began to think he might lose his balance and fall over if he did not move again soon. Then, as quickly as they had stopped, Grandfather and Uncle Royce moved forward again in unison. The Boy did not move a muscle until Grandfather lowered his hand. He took a breath and with a forward step, regained confidence of his balance again.

The three moved at a much slower pace now. In slow motion, the hunt had begun. Every three or four steps, Grandfather and Uncle Royce froze. The Boy almost overstepped the first couple of times and then learned the rhythm. Each time Grandfather looked down at the Boy's boots, the Boy became more aware that he needed to be sure he was picking up his feet between steps and planting them firmly heel to toe. The Boy had been warned about dragging his feet and this extra effort seemed to give him back some control of the clumsy fitting boots.

At one point during a pause, Grandfather gestured down to the ground in front of them. When the Boy looked down, Grandfather directed him to a large fresh buck track and then showed the Boy the others to either side. The tracks, hoof prints, were large, and to illustrate how big the animal was Uncle Royce pulled the air above his head to the length of his arm and then rolled his hand in a crescent to signify a large rack. Then Uncle Royce pointed into the woods from where the tracks had come, with a fluid motion he traced the animal's path across the road in front of them and into the thicket on the other side, moving his hand forward to show the buck would be circling back around to the trail. Grandfather nodded his head in agreement. Since the buck had crossed recently, they could expect so see him enter the trail again at any time. The three went forward. The Boy was more cautious than before. With each step, the Boy scanned the darkness before him for the buck and the ground below for more tracks.

The rhythm of the hunt was sedating, captivating, and the Boy's senses were becoming keen. He could hear crackles echoing through the woods and took notice of where little voles had run alongside the edge of the two-track.

The two-track was opening up now and the trees to his right were becoming hardwoods while to his left a thicket bordering the trail continued. Then, when the Boy noticed the buck's tracks coming back onto the trail at the same time as the elders, his chest filled again. He now moved in accord with the older men. He stopped when they stopped, looked when they looked, and listened when they listened. As they continued ahead, the buck's tracks stayed on the two-track. Only moments before, the buck had walked along the same path that he walked now. The Boy was certain that with more light he could see the buck in front on them. They were careful in their stealth and there was no breeze. The buck would have no way of knowing the three were following behind. If a smell lingered at all, the scent would be of apples.

Wanting to catch up with the buck, the Boy focused on the trail in front of him, gradually less mindful of his surroundings. He startled to a sudden thundering to his right. He turned in time to see a cackling pheasant loudly ruffle thick tail feathers as the large bird shuffled past them from under a small snow covered shrub. The three of them froze, knowing the pheasant had given away their position. When they were ready to go again, Uncle Royce turned his head, a toothy smile on his big round face, and though his features were dull in the light, the Boy thought Uncle Royce had comically lifted his brow. Uncle Royce was between the Boy and the edge of the trail where the pheasant had flushed and his smile told the Boy the older men had been just as easily shaken. The pheasant was a good reminder that with each further step, the three should not let the buck prints distract them from the greater woods.

The thicket eventually pulled to the left, opening to a small clearing on the side of the trail. After so many short steps and pauses, the Boy was not sure how far back they had come. A long time had passed since they left the ridge. There were times along the trail where the three had stood motionless until the Boy thought he could stand still no more. When they got to the center of the newly found clearing, Grandfather stopped, so the Boy stopped as well. Uncle Royce kept following the two-track and the buck's tracks that ran along the side. Grandfather emptied the carrots he was carrying on the ground, then took the burlap apple sack from the Boy, dumped the contents on top of the carrots, and with his heel, mashed them together. The apples were small black rocks in the dim light. The orange of the carrots glowed faintly against the snow. The Boy thought they would be following Uncle Royce and the buck. Instead, Grandfather led him over to the hardwood side of the trail across frin the two-track. Grandfather stepped into the woods, turned back to the Boy, raised his finger to his lips, and then beckoned the Boy forward.

Dead leaves from the elms and maples covered the ground, their brown and red edges curling up through the snow. To walk over the leaves silently was near impossible. The two did not have to go far. Among the maples stood an ancient pine, the boughs thick and heavy. Beneath the pine, two large roots ran outward from the trunk in a huge semicircle hugging a sunken hollow. At the base of the trunk was a red heat seat, the same Uncle Royce carried, and one of the blue vinyl seat cushion life preservers with straps sewn onto the sides from Grandfather's boat. Neither were touched by snow. Under the cushions, an old quilt and cloth sleeping bag fanned out into the hollow, disappearing under pine needle and leaves.

Hunched under the large boughs, Grandfather entered the womb of the tree, set his rifle against the trunk, and gently shook out the quilt and sleeping bag. Grandfather arranged the cushions and blankets together in a nest and then waved the Boy over. The Boy nestled against the base on the cushions and thick sleeping bag. The trunk contoured comfortably against his back. Grandfather rested next to him, pulled the quilt over their legs, and eased his rifle onto his lap. The smell of mildew from the blankets was familiar, no different than the cushions in the van, only now there was the addition of rotting leaves. Grandfather appeared to be very comfortable hidden in the camouflaged bed. The Boy imagined that his family had tucked themselves into this very same bed of decay for years, for generations.

In the middle of the clearing, the Boy could make out the dark stain of carrots and apples where they had kicked up the snow. Grandfather tapped the Boy on the shoulder and gave him another hard candy. As the Boy carefully unwrapped the candy, gently squeezing the sweet from between the wax paper, Grandfather put two fingers to his eyes and then pointed to the right and to the left and then to the right again. The Boy understood. His body locked in place, he began to scan back and forth, slowly and continuously, his head a beacon planted low in the tree. He sucked slowly on the candy. With his right arm, the only other part of his body with any mobility besides his head, the Boy was unsure if he could easily lift and point the shotgun that resting across his lap when the time came.

The Boy's breath was heavy.

Except for the clearing, the Boy could not really make out anything else around him. Even the two-track they had walked in on had disappeared into a vague bluish darkness at the clearing's edge. The path out and further back where

Uncle Royce had ventured were dark voids in the surrounding thicket. The contrast of the indigo twilight darkened the shadows within the hardwoods.

When the snow began to fall, the woods became even darker.

In paying so much attention to the open patch of snow before him and the dark recesses of the trees to his sides, the Boy had not taken notice that Grandfather was sleeping until he heard the unmistakable deep wheezing breaths threatening to become snores. Suddenly alone, the depths surrounding him took new meaning. Not wanting to shirk his duty, the Boy peered ever harder into the snowy twilight. The billowy, wet flakes tricked the corners of his eyes. At one point, he was sure the silhouette of a giant buck leapt high into the clearing, disappeared, reappeared, continuing to do so again and again in the mist. Loud thwacks from behind the pine occasionally broke the stilled silence and with each sudden sound, the Boy would hold his breath, expecting a deer to parade toward him. That never happened and as Grandfather slept, the Boy's tenacity waned.

A shiver forced his shoulders tight, the cold had found the Boy. Again, parts of his body were too hot, while his face and neck grew cold. The Boy drew a deep and shuddering breath and, not wanting to risk moving his arm, burrowed his chin under his coat.

The sun rose above the snow clouds. The lightness of day gradually brightened the woods. The sky grew more distinct and the silhouettes of the trees sharpened. Red brambles started to dominate the thicket. Pinecones, shadows a short time before, developed more detail and the Boy could now make out the tongued wooden leaves spread open and bare.

Above the feed pile, the Boy could see the flakes of snow appear from loftier heights than before. The snow fell swiftly in spirals and the air grew heavy and moist. As the apples grew more definitive, he could see that the carrots below them were almost entirely buried. How long they had been laying beneath the pine the Boy did not know. A long time, judging by the worn out repetition of turning to the left and to the right. He tried to decide if the apples and carrots were as he and his Grandfather had left them, or if somehow an animal, maybe a rabbit and not a deer, had snuck in the during the last looming darkness and stirred the pile. He expected Uncle Royce to, at any moment, come walking up the two-track, which he could now make out clearly. He found himself anticipating Uncle Royce more than a deer. In addition, the silence was becoming unbearable and he was hungry. His thoughts raced about getting back to the van and to the warm fire at his grandparents' house. A deep sigh overtook him that turned into a silent yawn, forcing his jaw open and making his eyes wet.

The romance of the hunt sounded far more exciting than what the Boy was experiencing. The forest behind him now, vast in his sight, was empty and still, save for the movement of the falling snow. The predatory leer from twilight had shifted to a restless gaze. The Boy lost himself deep into the trees, pondering that this part of the farm was all new to him.

The Boy's duty had become his burden, monotony the morning mainstay.

If the Boy's family had sat beneath this tree for generations, they did so out of boredom. Other boys in school talked of hunting as an active sport, spending the day marching through forests and swamps. The Boy knew that despite the few who chased dogs during bear and raccoon season, the majority spent sunup and dusk sitting as he was now, waiting for a buck to grace their presence as a target. No wonder there were so many arrowheads peppering the woods, the Indians surely would have driven themselves batty with endless days of sitting. The Boy resolved that at least he only had to go out one time a year. He would only have to do this for another two weeks. Unless, of course, he actually saw something first. He was not sure if he would be able to sit out the rest of the season. Maybe he would get lucky. He decided that after all of the preparation, the careful steps, the stillness to paralysis, what really mattered was luck. If he had the tenacity to sit there in one place, eventually, imminently, a deer would walk up.

No wonder Grandfather insisted on having only one shell. The Boy was now convinced Grandfather was absolutely right, you did not need more than one shell if you had a sure shot, because the sure shot was the easy part, waiting for the opportunity to shoot was what was so hard.

With the light came sound, the woods began to click and crackle. A whippoorwill bid good morning to the world deep in the thicket across the clearing and a woodpecker searched for breakfast high up in a hardwood behind him. A little chickadee landed on the edge of the pine bough then hopped to Grandfather's lap and then onto the barrel of the 300. The Boy looked at the bird watching Grandfather, now lightly snoring. He heard a crackle to his other side and saw another chickadee balancing on the branch of a very small tree. The ice and snow fell from the branch as the chickadee moved down the length. The little chickadees, with their chubby breasts and black hooded caps, were playful and the Boy found them entertaining as they hopped about the small trees and his blanket apron.

The day was getting warmer and the smell of the woods changed with the morning from stale to fresh, most likely from the new fallen snow that was now becoming a gray cloud of flurries. The Boy did not realize how heavy the snow was falling until, to his right, he saw Uncle Royce marching down the two-track, splotchy as a backdrop to the mass of snow. The Boy turned to tap Grandfather. To the Boy's surprise, Grandfather was already leaning forward, pulling the blanket from his waist.

"Let's go, son," said Grandfather.

Uncle Royce waited in front of them as they exited the hardwoods.

Standing in the open clearing, the Boy stretched. The world was brighter, larger, and magical. A different world than the one he had entered earlier this morning, with fluffy snow now covering every surface. Up the trail from where Uncle Royce had come, he could see a larger clearing a short distance away, and the hardwoods from which he had stepped appeared expansive. The feed pile was mostly covered now. The Boy noticed that the small clearing was cut purposely square into the thicket, and if a cement birdbath was plopped in the center, the glade could easily pass for a side garden courtyard.

The posture of Uncle Royce and Grandfather was relaxed and casual and they spoke in low tones, subdued by the tranquility of the woods and not the hunt. Uncle Royce's exit signaled that the window of opportunity to see a deer had closed, the does and bucks alike would be down for morning naps, their nocturnal roaming completed.

"Did you hear him?" asked Grandfather.

"He was moving around the edge of the woods, back and forth, all morning," said Uncle Royce. "Two does came into the end of the field and I thought he would follow, but he didn't. I took a walk back there before coming out and I could see his tracks by the edge of the trees. He must have just been watching them."

"He's big?"

"I saw a rub this high up," Uncle Royce held his hand level to his face, "He's big all right."

The Boy was impressed with Uncle Royce's account. Uncle Royce had actually seen deer.

Nothing had happened near them.

The three hunters headed out of the clearing back up the two-track toward the van. They walked at a casual pace, without the pause they had hiked in with. The sides of the two-track, a tunnel now roofed by the flurried snow, were walled by the brown, red, and grey thicket. The Boy could see into the hardwoods to the side for a while, a view that diminished when they got into the evergreens. Grandfather and Uncle Royce conversed about work that needed to be done in the garage back at the house. The Boy was not paying too much attention. He continued to occasionally freeze, distracted by visceral sounds brought on by the hypersensitivity of sitting long and quiet. The older men kept going forward at a constant pace so that the Boy had to catch up after each break.

Getting to the mouth of the trail did not take them long. The trail quickly opened up onto the ridge. Uncle Bob's car was parked next to the van and Uncle Bob and Uncle Dick were leaning on the hood drinking coffee out of thermos lid cups. Uncle Bob had removed his coat and looked as relaxed as if he were sitting on a sofa. Uncle Dick was smoking a cigarette, something he obviously had been waiting to do all morning. Though the Boy could see them talking, he could not hear them until he was close.

"How'd you do?" asked Grandfather.

"Well," said Uncle Bob in a slow drawl, "I sat on that tree stump by the pit and I thought I saw a rack bouncing back through the swamp but…" he shrugged his shoulders.

Grandfather looked over to Uncle Dick. Uncle Dick shook his head and in his deep voice said, "I was sitting in the orchard, but when the snow came I couldn't see anything. So I walked the edge of the property and saw tracks where they were hopping back and forth over the fence." Uncle Dick held his hand out flat, his eyes as wide a quarters, "Look at this, they could have been right there in front of me and I wouldn't have seen 'em. Not in this."

The men laughed and so did the Boy. He was not sure if Uncle Dick was serious, but Uncle Dick's booming voice and matter of fact way of speaking were funny.

"Am I right?" asked Uncle Dick. He then turned to the Boy, "How did you do?"

The Boy had not thought what to say, he did not expect to be asked. "I heard a lot of movement behind me," said the Boy. The men looked at him earnestly, "but when it got light, all I could see were these chickadees bouncing all over, making all kinds of racket."

Uncle Bob joined in, "Those little buggers, they wouldn't leave me alone. On my shoulders, on my feet, I had one on my boot that I kept shaking off and he just kept coming back."

Hearing his Uncle's animated response pleased the Boy and he joined Grandfather and his great uncles in laughter. There were moments the Boy had felt alone in the woods and he now knew that the older men had been there with him, sharing his experience.

"I'm surprised your grandfather's snoring didn't scare everything away, I could hear him all the way across the ridge," said Uncle Bob.

The Boy's eyes opened wide.

"Sounded like a saw from where I was," said Uncle Royce. The corners of Uncle Royce's mouth dug high into his round cheeks. Uncle Royce nodded to the Boy. At first, the Boy had thought they were joking then quickly caught on that Grandfather's habits were legend. The Boy smiled in turn. Grandfather said nothing.

"All right, let's get back to the house," said Grandfather. He stepped up to the van and opened the side door.

The Boy knew what to do. He pumped the shotgun to expel his cartridge onto the ground. The shell disappeared beneath the snow. He pumped the twelve-gauge a few more times to be sure the gun was unloaded. He fished the red shell out of the snow and then stepped over to the van to slide the gun into the leather case.

Grandfather and Uncle Royce left their rifles loaded.

Grandfather and Uncle Royce set their rifles on top of the open gun cases and then proceeded to get into the van. The Boy did not understand at first why the rifles were still loaded until, instead of driving directly out to the road, Grandfather circled the ridge. In a final sweep, they were looking for signs of movement in the corners of the field where the deer were known to nap in the morning. At the mouth of the road, they unloaded their rifles outside the van. When Grandfather was back behind the wheel, Uncle Bob and Uncle Dick led the way back down the bumpy gravel two-track toward the entrance of the farm.

The Boy bounced on the bed in the back of the van and cast off his cap and gloves. The cold air from the fan felt warm after being out in the woods.

* * * * *

* * * * *

THE END

* * * * *

ABOUT THE AUTHOR

Daniel Arthur Smith is the author of the international bestsellers THE CATHARI TREASURE, THE SOMALI DECEPTION, and a few other novels and short stories.

He was raised in Michigan and graduated from Western Michigan University where he studied meta-physics, cognitive science, philosophy, and comparative religion. He began his career as a bartender, barista, poetry house proprietor, and teacher, and then became a technologist and futurist for the Fortune 100 across the Americas and Europe.

Daniel has traveled to over 300 cities in 22 countries, residing in Los Angeles, Kalamazoo, Prague, Crete, and now writes in Manhattan where he lives with his wife and young sons.

* * * * *